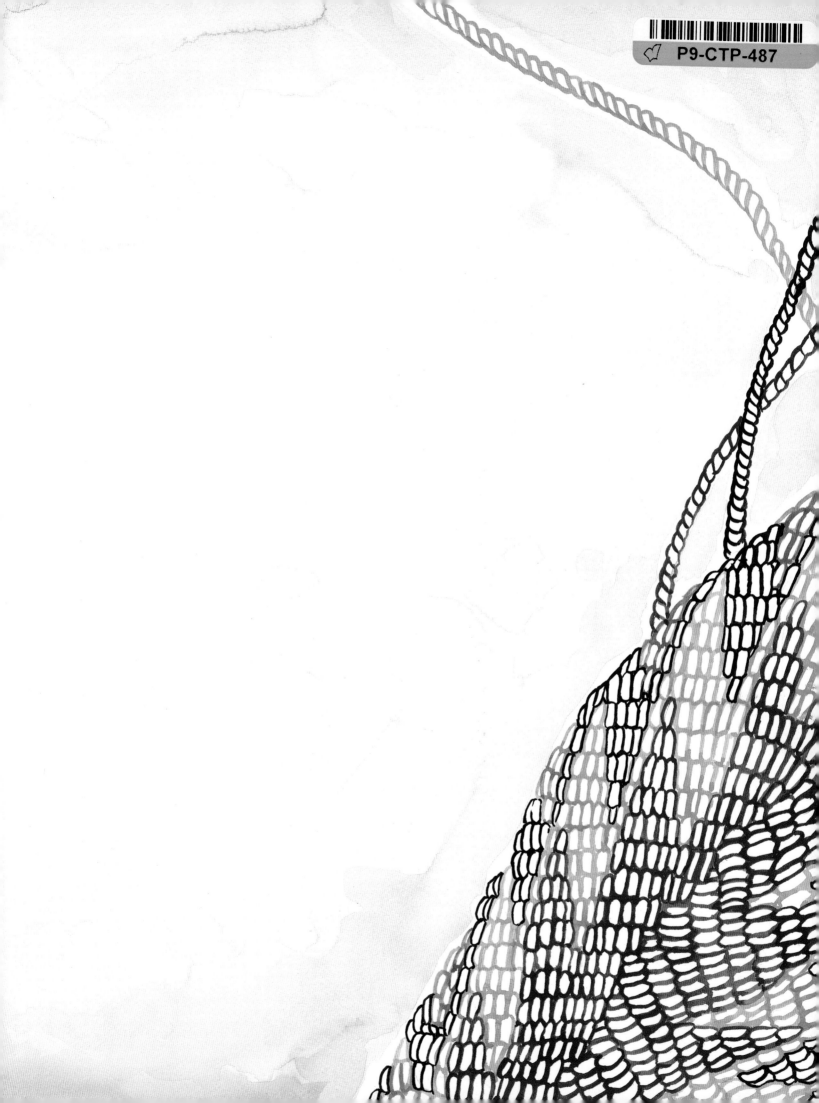

For Native veterans, those in active duty, their loved ones and the Native Nations they all come from—GV (wado) thank you.
–T.S.

To my grandmother Vera and my mom, who wove a deep love for creating with my hands when I was very young.
–W.A.

KOKILA
An imprint of
Penguin Random House LLC, New York

Text copyright © 2019 by Traci Sorell • Illustrations copyright © 2019 by Weshoyot Alvitre

Printed in China • ISBN 9780735230606

10 9 8 7 6 5 4 3 2 1
Design by Jasmin Rubero • Text set in P22 Underground Medium

CIP Data is available

This art was created with gouache, watercolor, and ink on illustration board.

AT THE MOUNTAIN'S BASE

by Traci Sorell

illustrated by

Weshoyot Alvitre

Kokila

At the mountain's base

grows a hickory tree.

Beneath this sits a cabin.

In that cabin

lies a cozy kitchen,

where a stove's fire warms.

On that stove

simmers savory goodness
in well-worn pans.

By those pans
sits a grandma,
weaving.

And worrying.

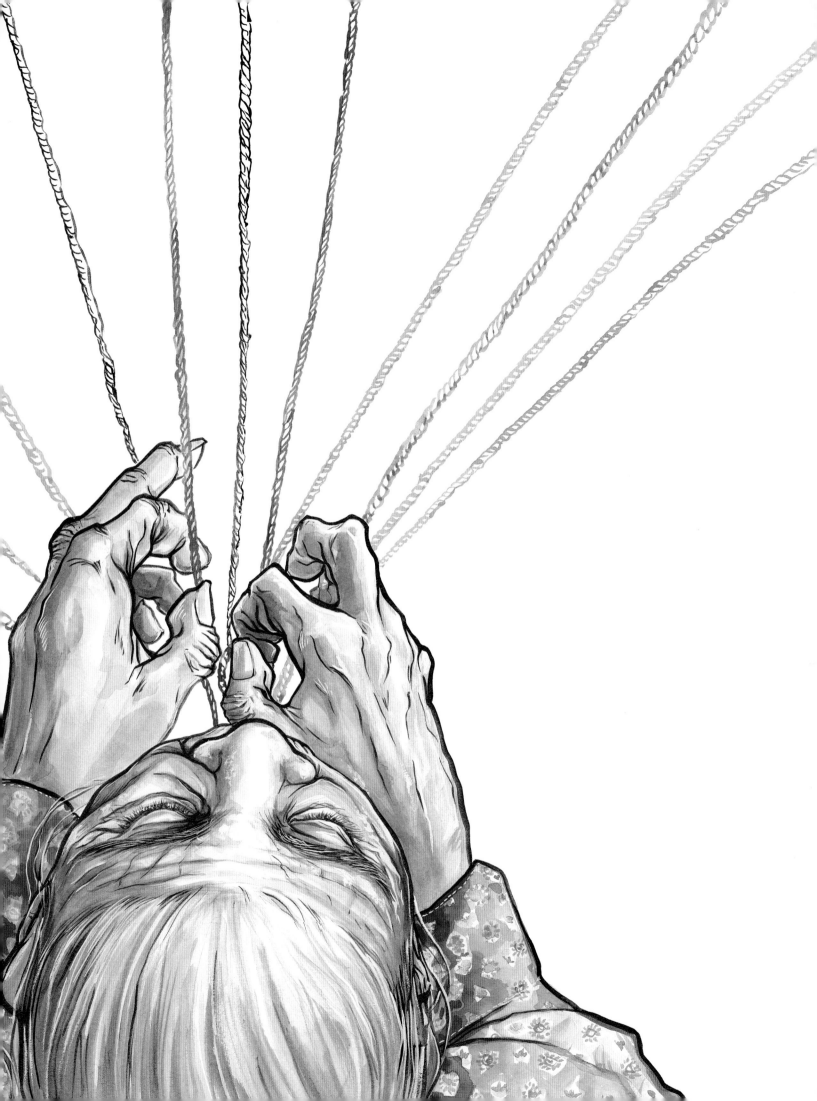

Around that grandma
gathers a family,
tending and singing.

Within their song

unfolds a battle,

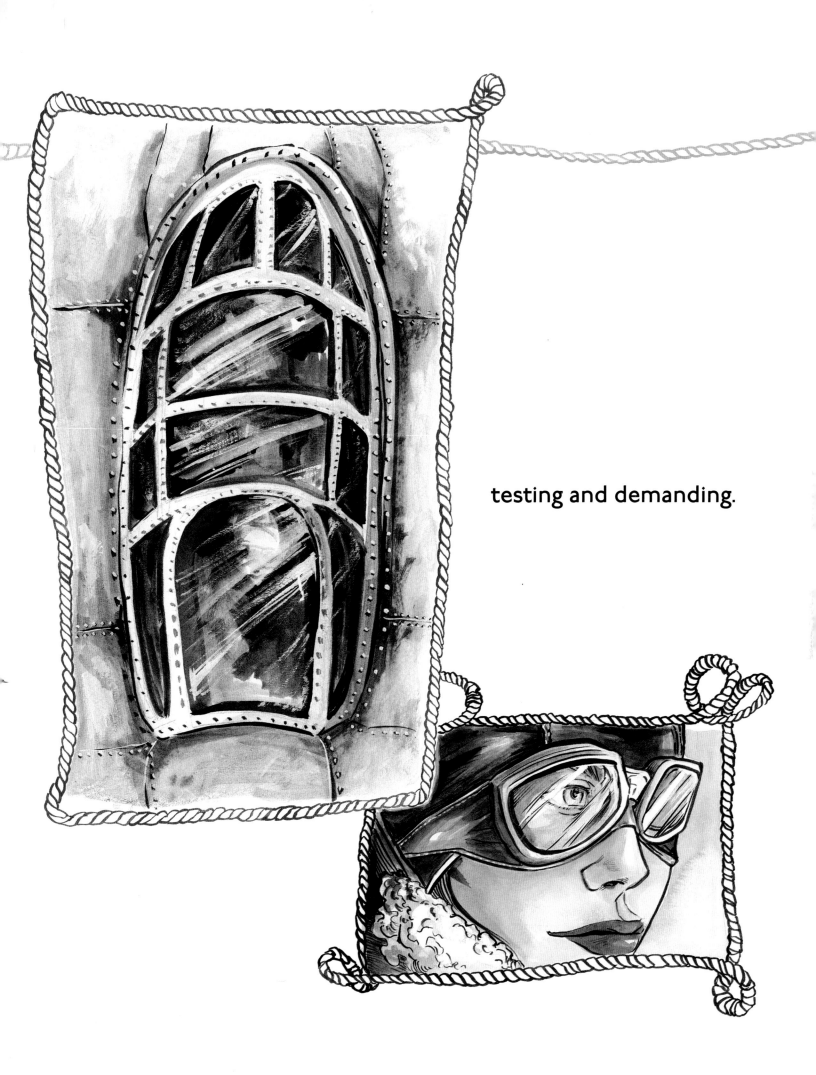

testing and demanding.

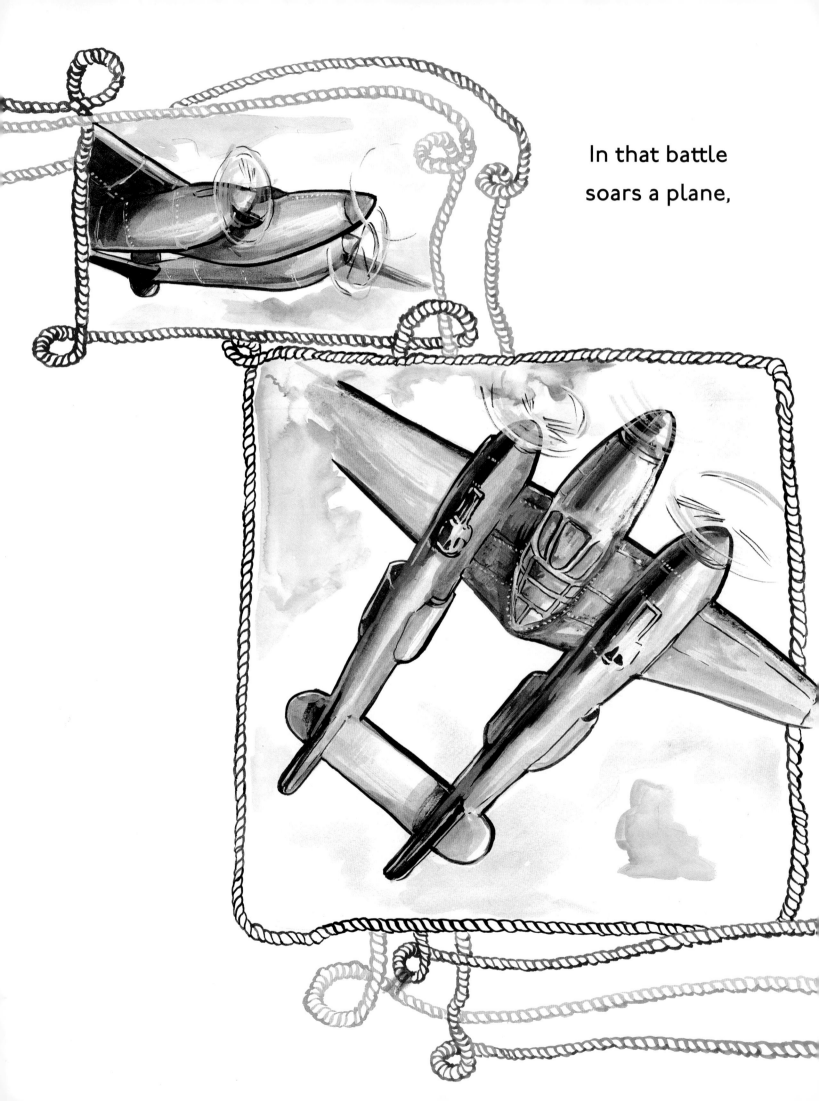

In that battle
soars a plane,

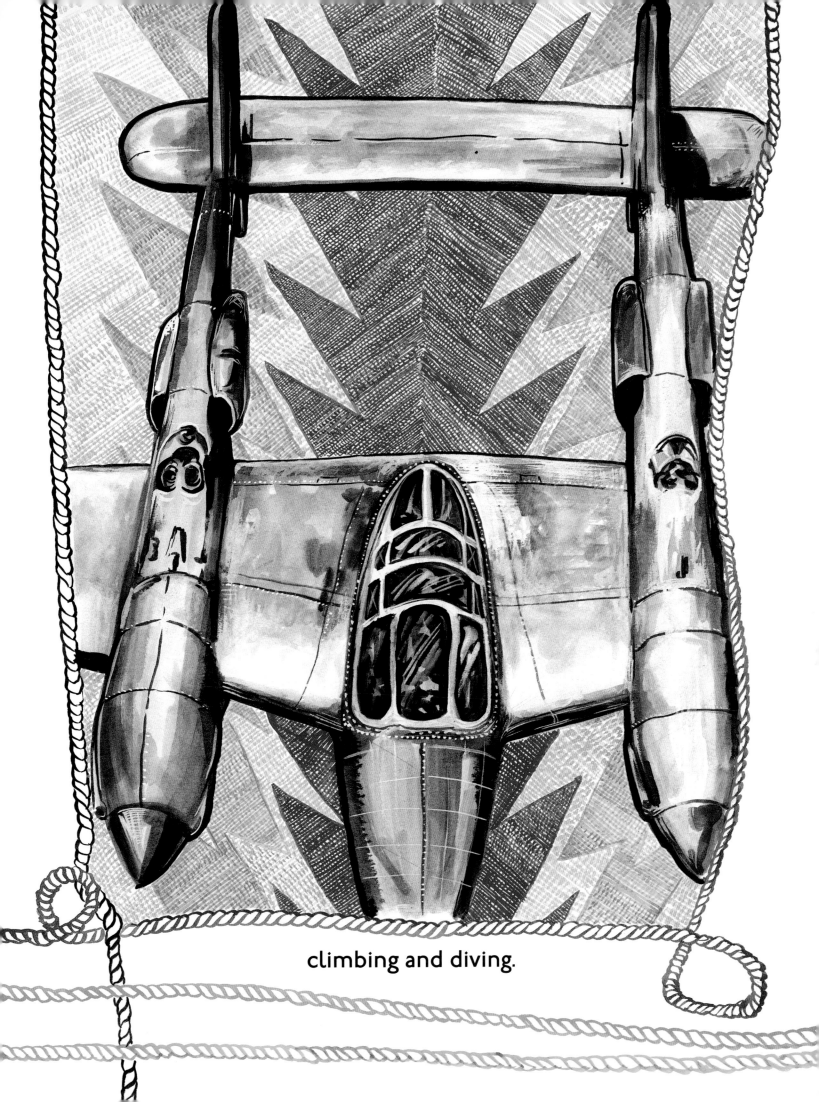

climbing and diving.

Inside that plane
flies a pilot,
protecting and defending.

Within that pilot
forms a prayer,

pleading for peace.

Because at the mountain's base,

beneath the hickory tree,

sits a cabin.

And in that cabin
huddles a family,
waiting for her return.

AUTHOR'S NOTE

Although this poem is about a fictional Cherokee family, Native women have served and continue to serve in wars while receiving strong support from their families. Women from American Indian and Alaska Native Nations have served in intertribal conflicts, wars started by European colonizers fighting for territories claimed in North America, and later within the United States Armed Forces. More recently, these women serve at proportionately higher rates than all other Active Duty, Reserve, and National Guard Servicemembers.

One such woman was Ola Mildred "Millie" Rexroat, an Oglala Lakota pilot. The only Native woman among 1,074 Women Airforce Service Pilots (WASPs) in World War II, Millie risked her life towing targets for male student pilots to fire on for practice. She also transported nonflying personnel and cargo during the war. Then she served active duty in the Air Force Reserve during the Korean War as an air traffic controller. In 2009, she along with the other WASPs was awarded the Congressional Gold Medal, the highest award given by the U.S. Congress to individuals or groups worldwide for outstanding accomplishments and contributions. A few months after her death on June 28, 2017, the Ellsworth Air Force Base in South Dakota renamed and dedicated a building in her honor.